W9-BFS-751

# Hurry up, Franklin

For Brooke and Devin – P.B.

For Jack and Beth,
with love – B.C.

*Library of Congress Cataloging-in-Publication Data*

Bourgeois, Paulette.
    Hurry up, Franklin.

    Originally published: Toronto: Kids Can Press, 1989.
    Summary: Even though he is very slow and has many
distractions on the way, Franklin the turtle manages to
get to Bear's house just in time for a special event.
    [1. Turtles–Fiction.   2 Animals–Fiction.
3. Parties–Fiction]   I. Clark, Brenda, ill.   II Title.
PZ7.B6654Hu  1990      [E]      89-10246
ISBN 0-590-42620-6

12 11 10 9 8 7 6 5 4 3 2        0 1 2 3 4 5/9

Printed in the U.S.A.                             36
First Scholastic printing, January 1990

# Hurry up, Franklin

*Written by* Paulette Bourgeois
*Illustrated by* Brenda Clark

SCHOLASTIC
HARDCOVER

SCHOLASTIC INC. ° New York

FRANKLIN could slide down a river bank all by himself. He could count forwards and backwards. He could zip zippers and button buttons. He could even sleep alone in his small, dark shell. But Franklin was slow…

Even for a turtle.

"Hurry up, Franklin," pleaded his mother. "Hurry up, Franklin," begged his father. "Hurry up, Franklin," shouted his friends.

"I'll be there in a minute," said Franklin. But there was always so much to see and so much to do. Franklin was never there in just a minute.

One day Franklin was very excited. He was going to Bear's house. It was a special day. A very special day. "Hurry up," said Franklin's mother. "You can't be late."

It wasn't far to Bear's house. Just along the path, over the bridge and across the berry patch. Franklin meant to hurry – except he saw something unusual. He wandered off the path and found Rabbit bobbing up and down in the tall, green grass.

"What are you doing?" Franklin asked Rabbit.

"Playing Leap Frog," said Rabbit. "Do you want to play with me?"

"I'm on my way to Bear's house," said Franklin. "And I can't be late."

"There's lots of time," said Rabbit, forgetting that Franklin was slow, even for a turtle. "It's just along the path, over the bridge and across the berry patch. Come and play with me."

Franklin knew it wasn't far and so he said yes. Rabbit leaped over Franklin again and again. But after a while Rabbit said, "It's time to go. Hurry up, Franklin, or you'll be late." Then Rabbit bounded along the path on his way to Bear's house.

"I'll be there in a minute," said Franklin. And he meant to be there in just a minute – except he heard an odd sound. Franklin wandered even farther off the path until he found Otter sliding up and down the river bank.

"What are you doing?" Franklin asked Otter.

"Slipping and sliding," answered Otter. "Do you want to play with me?"

"I'm on my way to Bear's house," said Franklin. "And I can't be late."

"There's lots of time," said Otter, forgetting that Franklin was slow, even for a turtle. "It's just along the path, over the bridge and across the berry patch. Come and play with me."

Franklin knew it wasn't far and so he said yes. Franklin slid down the river bank and splashed and blew bubbles until Otter said, "It's time to go. Hurry up, Franklin, or you'll be late." Then Otter swam away with a flick of her tail on her way to Bear's house.

"I'll be there in a minute," said Franklin.

It was very quiet. Franklin was alone and far from the path. Rabbit had gone. Otter had gone. Franklin had a frightening thought. Maybe he was already too late!

Franklin walked as fast as his turtle legs could walk. He hurried through the fields and along the path. He was almost at the bridge when he heard a rustle in the grass and saw a patch of reddish fur. It was Fox, hiding in the brush.

"Do you want to play with me?" asked Fox.

"I have to hurry," said Franklin. "I'm on my way to Bear's house!"

"It's not very far," said Fox. "Just over the bridge and across the berry patch. Come and play hide and seek."

Franklin hesitated. Hide and seek was his favorite game.

"Ready or not?" asked Fox.

Franklin shouted, "Ready!" And he was just about to step off the path when he remembered it was a very special day and he couldn't be late.

"I can't play," said Franklin. "I have to hurry."

Franklin rushed along the path and over the bridge. He was in such a hurry that he almost stepped on Snail.

"Where are you going in such a hurry?" asked Snail, who was even slower than Franklin.

"I'm on my way to Bear's house," said Franklin. "I have to hurry. I can't be late. Being late would ruin everything."

Snail began to cry.

"What's wrong?" asked Franklin.

"I'll never get to Bear's house on time," sobbed Snail.

"It's not very far," said Franklin. "Just across the berry patch."

It seemed very far to Snail, and he sobbed even harder.

"Don't worry," said Franklin bravely. But even Franklin was worried. It was farther than he thought. It was a very big berry patch. He wished he hadn't played with Rabbit. He wished he hadn't played with Otter. He wished he hadn't wasted so much time talking to Fox. Then he remembered it was Bear's special day. There was no time to cry. He had to hurry.

"Come along, Snail," said Franklin, helping Snail slide onto his back.

"Please hurry," whispered Snail. But Franklin needed no urging. He moved surely and steadily. He hurried past the blackberries. He hurried past the gooseberries. He even hurried past the raspberries. And he was almost at Bear's front gate when he remembered something important.

He stopped right there at the edge of the berry patch and started picking handfuls of the ripest, plumpest, juiciest blueberries in the berry patch.

"We don't have time to pick berries," said Snail. "You know we can't be late."

Franklin whispered into Snail's right ear. And soon Snail was helping too. They picked until the bush was clean.

"Hurry up," said Snail. "Please hurry up, Franklin."

He hurried up Bear's path, through the front door, across the kitchen and into Bear's living room.

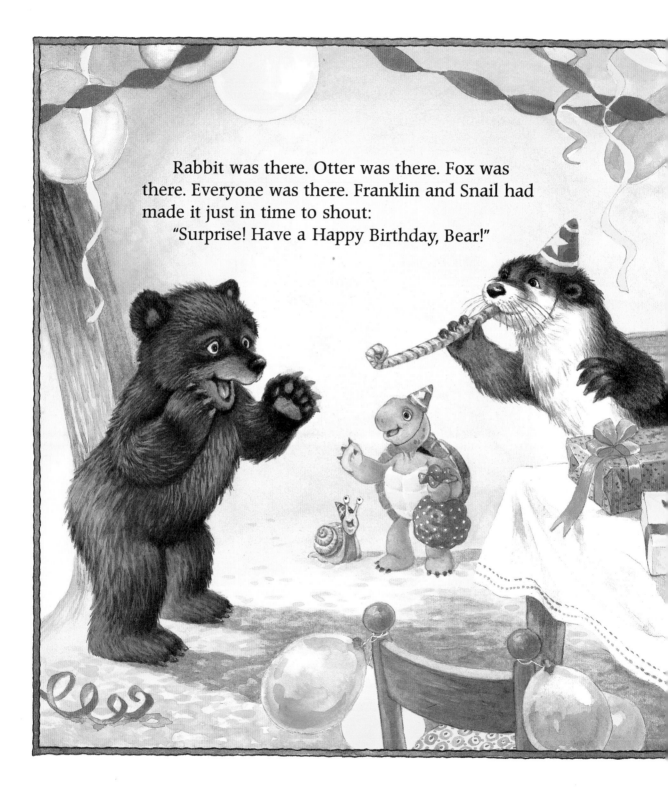

Rabbit was there. Otter was there. Fox was there. Everyone was there. Franklin and Snail had made it just in time to shout:
"Surprise! Have a Happy Birthday, Bear!"

And he did.